Little Ricky
The Boy from Otter Lake
Wise Mothers and Forgiving Grandmothers

Richard J.M. Gauthier

Copyright © 2023 Richard J.M. Gauthier

All rights reserved.

ISBN: 9798397066143

DEDICATION

To my sister Audrey,
who encouraged me to write.
To those I have met along
my writing journey,
who encouraged me to continue.

This short story is one of the twelve tales from Gauthier's first collection called "Little Ricky the Boy from Otter Lake". The complete first collection is an assortment of a dozen charming fictional, heartwarming short stories that are well-suited for children, and children of all ages! Travel through the seasons and special events from a time when life was simpler, and days were filled with love, support, and happiness.

From his amazing birth to the proud age of five, discover the fun, the life lessons, the love, and the laughter as only can be experienced from a child's perspective.

CONTENTS

Acknowledgments   i

Story Number 2 – Little Ricky – Wise Mothers and Forgiving Grandmothers   1
A little boy's curiosity with Mother Nature gets him into trouble, but family matriarchs teach him life lessons.

ACKNOWLEDGMENTS

A huge thank you to my editor
and proofreader.
Pierre-Paul Lacroix

Little Ricky

Wise Mothers and Forgiving Grandmothers

Little Ricky – Wise Mothers and Forgiving Grandmothers

The day arrived with warm and bright sunshine. Each of the rear and shop-side windows of the family home streamed in beautiful sparkling light on this chilly, but fresh spring morning. He awoke slowly from his restful sleep, and at the teasing of the sunlight on his face, he opened his big hazel eyes and fluttered his dark long lashes. Though still sleepy, he wiggled and stretched out in bed and turned to look out the window. He loved the morning. To greet the new morning, he put his gaze upon a magical view from the bedroom window. The early sky was angel blue and big, white, fluffy clouds drifted along softly throughout its heavenly vastness. The tall fir trees of the backyard glistened in the morning light. His ears took in the sounds of a gentle breeze rustling outside and that of the early day song of the robins. This little boy loved springtime. It was the time when the snow had now long melted, and the trees and grass were showing growth and green. The outside world was alive and this boy could not wait to get out there to enjoy it all!

This little lad was growing up and he was thrilled each day to experience more and more of God's beautiful world. He was now thirty-nine months old! Is that not what Mommy had told him just the night before? According to her, Veronica or Mommy to him, was well on her way to being 38 years old, but despite her baby's older age in number of months at 39, than her age in years at 37, she teased him that even though he was now 3 years, and 3 months old, he was still her big baby and he still needed to go to bed when told. She explained to him that bedtime was the best time for little boys, because it was while in bed and asleep that growing-up happened. She insisted that bedtime and sleep was also the most fun time for little boys, because that is when the thrill and adventure of dreams came about to fill their nights with amusement and fun. Ricky knew Mommy was correct because she was very smart. In his view, all parents were very smart and he had intended to learn a lot from both Mommy and Daddy. The truth is, bedtime was not a big issue for little Ricky, because he felt safe and secure in his snug bed and did enjoy the fun of his many dreams.

This little fellow was indeed growing up. The youngest of five children, he now stood nearly three feet tall and had a healthy weight of just under thirty pounds. His rounded face was handsome. It featured dark thick eyebrows, large hazel eyes that sparkled with golden flecks, long curled eyelashes, and a strong nose set between two chubby cheeks; each of which were completely covered in a heavy sprinkling of freckles. His mouth was full with healthy rose coloured lips. His little chin stuck out slightly which was a good thing, because it reduced the size and girth of his chubby little neck. His frame was smaller than that of most boys his age, but he did not seem to lack strength or energy. Today, he tumbled quickly out of bed with a thump. He swiftly tugged the bed covers and gave them a yank. Surely he thought, this would wake his older brother Bernie with whom he shared one of the two double beds in the boys' room. The other bed was shared, on the other side of the room by his middle brothers Chris and Brian. With a quick glance towards their bed, he confirmed that both brothers were already awake and gone. He was sure they were already downstairs and helping with the breakfast. Bernie, on the other hand, was still stretched out in bed and half asleep. Ricky tugged at the blankets once more and then shook the bed as hard as he could. "Hey Bernie, it's time to get up", he hollered. Bernie turned, smiled at his brother and said, "Hey give me another five minutes will you. Go downstairs and let me have five more Zs. I am older and need more sleep!"

Ricky quickly put on his pants, grabbed a sweater and left the room. At the top of the stairs in the upstairs hallway, a glance down the hall told him that Mommy, Daddy, and his sister were also already awake as well, confirmed by open doors to their respective bedrooms. As luck would have it, in a family of eight individuals, no light shone from under the bathroom curtain at this time, confirming it was free. "Yeah", he hummed to himself. "It is free! It is a place we all need to use, but with seven others in the house, it's a place hard to find free", he giggled. So, he skipped down the hall and entered the bathroom. After a short while, he exited feeling refreshed with an empty bladder and freshly washed hands and face. His tummy now grumbled, so he scooted down the stairs as quickly as he could. It was time for breakfast and he knew something fresh, yummy, and filling would be ready. It was Mommy and his brothers who usually got the breakfast prepared, but on the weekends; especially on Sundays, it was Daddy who took over and treated everyone to a good fixing of bacon, fried eggs, and toast.

This morning, Saturday morning, it was Mommy who was the chief cook in the kitchen. She stood firmly at the big old wood stove as she stirred a fresh pot of oatmeal. "Well good morning lazy bones", she teased as she watched Ricky wobble onto the large wooden bench at the back of the table. "Are you hungry?" she asked. "Yes Mommy, I am hungry, but my bones are not lazy", he replied. "Well, you are the second last to get up Ricky, so your bones were lazy until just now", she chuckled. "Ahhhh no Mommy, I promise they are not lazy. It is Bernie who has the lazy bones because he is still in bed. His bones are much lazier than mine, because they are much bigger than mine", he quipped! Veronica laughed out loud because she had never heard that one before. "Ok, hush yourself and eat", she said. She brought the pot of porridge to the table and scooped out some into Ricky's waiting bowl. "Oh Mommy, that smells so good. I love hot-meal", he exclaimed. "No Ricky, it's not hot-meal, it is oatmeal", she corrected with a smile! Ricky grabbed the brown sugar bowl and put two big spoons full of the golden product over his oatmeal. He then reached for the milk pitcher and slowly poured some milk over top. The pitcher was brimming and heavy, so when he inadvertently spilled some of the milk over its top to the table, he quickly mopped it up with his sweater sleeve. "I spilled Mommy, but I caught it in time, this time", he said proudly! "Yes dear, but please do not use the sleeve of your sweater; next time, use the dish cloth like the rest of us! Ok Ricky?" Veronica cautioned. Ricky gulped shyly. "Yes Mother", he promised. "Ok, now hush yourself and eat up", his mother encouraged. "Daddy is already out in his shop. Your sister is out in the gardens helping your Granny, and Brian and Chris are already out cleaning up the wood chips in the wood shed", she continued. "What are you going to do today after your breakfast?" she inquired. The boy spooned some breakfast into his mouth, chewed slowly, swallowed, then responded "Mommy, I am going to do what I am the very best at. I am going to play and keep out of trouble". Veronica burst out a hearty laugh and said, "Keep out of trouble; well won't that be something new!" After breakfast Ricky found himself outside. He stood there at the back door, stretched his arms up as high as they could reach, and took in a deep gulp of fresh country air. He exhaled slowly and thought to himself on how he would spend the morning. How would he ensure that he fully completed his most important task of 'play'! The beautiful morning sun shone down upon him. Its rays warmed him and he felt energized. Under the warmth of the sun, suddenly, it came to him! He would go visit Mommy Robin, and check her nest to see if her pretty little blue eggs had turned into baby birds! As such, he made his way swiftly through the gardens taking care not to trample any of Granny's flowers, and plopped himself down under the big apple tree. He looked up. Mommy Robin had her nest way up there. This he knew for sure. His brother Chris had helped him take a peek the other day and had lifted him right up to the very branches that held the nest firmly in that tree. Ricky mused, how would he get way up there today without a boost from Chris? He considered, without help from anyone bigger than himself, how could he get way up there to look into that nest? Suddenly, it came to him! Of course, he would simply climb up the tree!

Next, he whistled loudly and hoped this would scare Mommy Robin off and away from her nest. He then grabbed a low branch in one hand, wrapped his little legs around the tree trunk and started to slowly hoist himself up. Up and up he went, using both his hands and feet to find, grasp, or step upon woody branches. He stopped for a bit to catch his breath. He was amazed and stunned by the beauty around him. The apple tree was a maze of intertwined branches filled with the lushest little green leaves. The smell was sweet and soft, and reminded Ricky of Granny's homemade applesauce. He was astounded at the sight of the soft pink and white blossoms. Surely, he thought to himself, this must be Heaven. After another few moments, he climbed higher, nearly to the top of the tree, and slowly approached the robin's nest. He quickly noted that Mrs. Robin was not home, a good thing when egg inspectors were about! Ricky pulled himself closer to the nest, but did not find beautiful blue eggs. Inside the nest instead were the tiniest, most ugly worm like creatures he had ever seen! "Oh", he exclaimed "Are these baby birds? Surely they are not, because they do not have many feathers" he said aloud! The little life forms started to peep, peep, peep and raise their little heads up with beaks wide open! "Wow", Ricky said! "Now is that not special", he exclaimed! He reached his hand up and over the nest to pet the little babies, when all of a sudden a quick swish and flap of wings of an angry mother came right at him.

The angry bird set upon his head and pecked down sharply with her beak. Then she started to scratch the boy's head in quite a flutter with her feet. Oh the pain thought Ricky! He could feel the jabs penetrate his skull. He thought she had broken through the bone of his skull and was pricking right into his brain! The bird suddenly whooshed away, but in an instant returned with hot fury. She flapped her wings hard, and then took a few nips at Ricky's ears. This time, her efforts were successful when suddenly Ricky lost his balance on his perch and he went tumbling quickly down from the tree with a loud bump, bump, snap, crack, bump, and crash!

The poor lad lay there flopped out at the bottom of the tree amongst the summer June rosebushes. He was winded, scratched up, and very sore. He slowly tried to move, but every little movement brought on more pain. He tried to reach out his arms to turn over onto his back, but pricks from sharp thorns on the rose canes and stems all around him dug into the skin of his arms and hands. He started to bleed, he felt very scared, and he started to cry. Within moments, he heard some rustling above him and soon realized that Granny had heard his cries and had come to comfort him or so he thought. "Oh you little rascal, what are you doing down there in my rosebushes", she inquired? Ricky sobbed and replied, "Granny I have fallen and I am bleeding." Granny knelt down and picked up the little guy in her strong arms and lifted him to safety. "What mischief have you been up to", she questioned? "I was just playing Granny. I climbed up your apple tree to visit Mrs. Robin. I wanted to play with her eggs. There were no eggs. They turned into baby birds", he explained. Granny examined the boy for serious injury. When she found none, she then examined the state of her beloved apple tree and her rose garden. "Oh you naughty boy, look at all the trouble you have caused", she scolded. "Oh Granny, but, but, but", Ricky stammered. "Will you look at the state of my beautiful rosebushes; they are all broken down and trampled on. Look at my poor apple tree. I planted that one from seed. You have broken that branch just there; so much that it will die and fall off", Granny cried. As she lowered Ricky to the ground, she pinched his ear and continued, "Go to the house now you little scamp and confess to your mother all the tomfoolery you have gotten yourself into". Ricky felt terrible that he had upset Granny so much that she too was now sobbing. He looked at her with sad eyes, eyes that were asking for forgiveness. His big hazel eyes welled up again with hot tears. Unfortunately, Granny was not yet in a forgiving mood. She pointed with a sharp finger toward the house and said, "To the house now Ricky, forgiveness will come later".

Ricky turned and ran towards the house. He stopped at the back door, yanked it open, and entered the kitchen. Mommy was there standing at the kitchen sink, just finishing up drying the dishes. When she saw the state of her little one, she quickly asked, "Good gracious Ricky, what happened to you?" "Oh Mommy, I fell from a tree and have greatly upset Granny", he wailed. Veronica knelt down beside her son, pulled him closer to her and inquired, "Are you hurt? Tell Mommy if anything hurts." "No Mommy, I am ok now. I just have a few scrapes from the rosebushes", he shared. "What were you doing in Granny's rosebushes", she asked? "Is that why Granny is cross with you", she questioned? Poor little Ricky knew he must tell the truth. After all, it was the only way. "Yes Mommy, that is why Granny is angry, but I was not playing in her roses. I promise I was not. I climbed up her apple tree. I wanted to see and play with Mrs. Robin's eggs. There were no eggs Mommy. They were replaced with tiny, tiny baby birds. They were like wet insects. I was just about to play with them, when Mrs. Robin attacked me. I think she picked my brains. It hurt so much, it made me fall. I fell into Granny's roses," Ricky declared. "Oh my, oh my", Veronica whispered. She examined the boy's head. "Despite the picking, I think your little brain will be fine, but tell me what on earth made you think it was safe to climb way up into Granny's tree", she inquired? "I do not know Mommy. I guess I was not thinking. I wanted to visit Mrs. Robin and felt that this was the best way to get way up there to her nest", he answered. "Well then, that is the lesson here Ricky. I know it is hard, even hard for me, but we must always try to think before we act! It is always worth taking the time to stop for a few moments and to choose the best and in your case safest action", she counseled. "Do you agree", she asked? "Yes Mommy, you are so smart. I agree with you. On thinking now, I should have asked one of my brothers to help me or perhaps could have used your small stepping ladder", he replied. "Yes Ricky that is correct. Always try to think things through to take the best steps possible and the safest; especially in your case my little Ricky", she quipped!

"Now listen Ricky, this is what we must do", she said. "First, let's get you up to the sink here and washed up. Then, I will put a Band-Aid on that little scrape. After that, I will give you a mug of tea and a cinnamon bun to take out to your Granny. We cannot have any disagreements between you and Granny. That will not do. You must ask her for forgiveness and share with her the lesson you have learned today. You shall sit with her and help her with whatever chores she needs doing until I have dinner ready for everyone. Is that a good plan Ricky", she asked? "Oh yes Mommy. I love Granny so much. I love you so much", he declared. He grasped his mother as firmly as he could with his little arms and hugged and hugged her.

Soon afterward, a happier little chap was washed up and on his way out to the gardens out back. In his hands, he carefully held a cup of tea and a little saucer holding a fresh cinnamon bun. He walked slowly this time to take care not to spill the tea or God forbid, to drop the sweet bun from its plate! From the garden gate at the back of the house, he strolled up the grassy pathway that separated two vegetable gardens, then turned right at the corner when he reached Mommy's main potato patch. He walked along this little stretch of path and then turned down again, this time towards Granny's flower and vegetable plots. There he found her, kneeling in the soil pulling out weeds from around new little sprouts. He was happy to see that her sweet sunny smile had returned to her face. He was happy to see that her tears had dried up.

Ricky approached his beloved grandmother and with his most angelic face, and his most atoned voice, he said to her, "Granny, I am very sorry for upsetting you earlier this morning. I am so truly sorry for hurting your apple tree and crushing down your beautiful roses. I know you work very hard to keep the gardens attractive and I was wrong to have been foolishly playing there. I sure hope your warm heart can forgive me", he pleaded. Granny looked at Ricky lovingly. Her eyes welled up with tears once more. She slowly raised herself up, dried her eyes and said, "Thank you Ricky. I am sorry as well for getting upset so quickly. Sometimes at my age, I forget what it is like to be a little one like you. I hope you can forgive me as well", she asked? "Yes Granny, there is enough forgiveness for both of us", he replied. "Look Granny, Mommy sent you a mid-morning treat to enjoy. I have tea and a silly bun for you", he exclaimed! Granny laughed and said, "So you have a "silly" bun do you? Well, I guess we will need to go over there under that tree in the shade, have a rest in my garden rocker, and share that delicious cinnamon bun!"

They made their way to the shade under the trees. Granny sat slowly, and then took her tea and bun from little Ricky. She put these securely on the little garden table beside her chair. She patted her leg and coaxed Ricky to jump up to sit upon her lap. "Ok, up you come", she encouraged. Ricky's smile beamed, as he grasped her waiting hand and boosted himself up upon her lap. Once comfortable, he turned to grasp her neck in a warm hug, and then he gave her a little kiss on her waiting cheek. "Granny, I truly love you. I am blessed to have you as my very best friend", Ricky sang. Granny smiled brightly, wiped her tears and said, "You are a little dear for sure, but tell me now, will you have a sip of tea and a taste of my "silly" bun?" "Yes Granny", Ricky replied. "However, I must first tell you all about a big lesson I learned today. I know from Mommy's and

Daddy's wise teachings that I am to learn from my mistakes. I made a mistake today by climbing your apple tree, without asking, without thinking. Today, Mommy helped me to see what I need to do to try to stay out of trouble", he continued. "You are becoming a wise young man early in your days", Granny responded. "Go on", she encouraged. "Well Mommy said and I agree; that to avoid finding trouble, which I usually do find, I must stop and think about what to do before doing it. By taking time to think, we can make better choices before we act! Mommy said, that it is always worth taking the time to stop and choose the best and safest action", he recited. Granny's whole being filled up with joy and love towards this little lad. She wrapped her arms around the little chap and gave him a tight granny hug. "Well Ricky, isn't it special that you continue to grow, grow both inside and out each day! Soon you will not be our little Ricky anymore, but will turn into a little man", Granny chimed. "Ahhh come on Granny, I will always be your little Ricky and I will always love you", he responded. "Ok Granny, it is time for your tea! It is getting cold and I want to have a big bite of your bun, as you promised", he teased! Granny laughed and said, "Who promised a "big" bite? Not this granny!"

The two friends happily enjoyed their little treat under the cool shade of the coniferous trees. They chatted and joked, and shared stories and secrets. The splendid morning weather continued with the sun rising higher in the sky. The clouds, though fewer now, still streamed softly across the blue heavens. The smell of apple blossoms perfumed the air. The scent of damp earth and fresh grass was the perfect complement to balance the sweetness of the blossoms. Suddenly, a Robin swooshed down from above and hopped along the grassy path beside the garden. "Look Ricky", Granny exclaimed. "Mrs. Robin has come to make peace with you as well", she whispered. "She is a good mother, like your Mommy, and I do hope her babies will be just as special as you are, our little Ricky!"

OTHER STORIES IN THE SERIES

Story Number 1 – Little Ricky – The Beginning
This is a tale of two anxious, but loving parents who welcome their new premature baby son into the world, during a frosty cold winter month of January.

Story Number 3 – Little Ricky – The Price for Sweets
A story portraying a father's deep forgiveness and a son's important early lesson that stealing does not pay.

Story Number 4 – Little Ricky – Easter Blessings
A quirky account of a little boy's Easter morning adventures with an eventual meeting of an inspirational young woman who encourages the boy to use his talents to their fullest; as she has with her beautiful singing abilities.

Story Number 5 – Little Ricky – Little Sprouts
A tale portraying a boy's love of family, home, and garden when all was supported by loving parents and a family that worked together to bring bounty to the table.

Story Number 6 – Little Ricky – A Day in Heaven on Earth
A boy's memory of a brisk walk with his mother through a beloved hometown with an ultimate crowning visit to two of the town's respected elders enabling a morning of fun, conversation, jokes, sweets, and shakers!

Story Number 7 – Little Ricky – A Jubilant July Visit
A story of a precious family visit from relatives who lived afar, which brought happiness and joy to a little boy during games, strolls in the forest, family meals, and banter and sharing between two young children.

Story Number 8 – Little Ricky – Veronica's Triumph
Summer is coming to an end quickly with the days of August flying by, however time remains for yet one more visit to Murray Lake for little Ricky and his kin at the family cottage. It is a beautiful adventure, but there is a catch!

Story Number 9 – Little Ricky – September School Saga!
This quirky tale unfolds to reveal the fears and joys of a boy's very first day of school. First impressions are lifelong impressions and little Ricky meets an early mentor when he is surprised by an amazing woman!

Story Number 10 – Little Ricky – Gentle Ghosts, Halloween Heist, and Perfect Pumpkins
A curious account that finds little Ricky intrigued by a true ghost story as he enjoys the fun and spooky events of Halloween night, a night that concludes with an affirmation of the boy's new beliefs that the dead are not truly departed!

Story Number 11 – Little Ricky – Remembrance, My Uncle Iggie, My Hero
A small boy, from a small town strives to better understand the meaning and history behind Remembrance Day Commemorations and what actually happened during the dark days of World War II. He consults his grandmother, mother, family correspondence, and a true veteran of the second Great War – his hero, his uncle.

Story Number 12 – Little Ricky – A Child's Magic Christmas
Christmas is drawing near, and a little child named Ricky becomes immersed in the special activities of the last few days before the big day. This special festive time of year is shared by him with both family and friends, but the most special thing of all is that he discovers the true secret of Santa Claus!

WHAT DID FANS HAVE TO SAY ABOUT RICK GAUTHIER'S FIRST BOOK LITTLE RICKY THE BOY FROM OTTER LAKE?

Eri rates Little Ricky the Boy from Otter Lake 5-STARS

Eri says: HEARTWARMING! The author skillfully brings you back in time to another era when life was simple, yet immensely with the love that builds a family. The book consists of separate tales recounted by the hero of the book, Rick Gauthier, known as Little Ricky by his family. An instant classic that will not disappoint! Written with heart and soul that shines through the pages.

Della rates Little Ricky the Boy from Otter Lake 5-STARS

She says: The unassuming nature of a young boy growing up in a rural setting. I really enjoyed the book. It really captured this young boy's wonderment, inquisitiveness and unspoiled nature. His appreciation and kindness are seen throughout the book in his interaction with his immediate family, relatives, and acquaintances.

An Amazon Customer rates Little Ricky the Boy from Otter Lake 5-STARS

She or he says: Very powerful story of a young boy's journey. A very enjoyable and easy read. The clever writing and pictures brought the book to life. The short stories are sure to put a smile on your face. A must read!

Floyd rates Little Ricky the Boy from Otter Lake 5-STARS

Floyd says: Read this book and wander off to a much simpler time. Wonderful book for youngsters. A little something to read to the little ones at bedtime. Chuck full of life lessons told in an easy to understand way. Read this book and wander off to a much simpler time.

Cathy rates Little Ricky the Boy from Otter Lake 5-STARS

Cathy says: A very unique retrospect of a young lad's loving upbringing in a small Pontiac, Quebec town. Very entertaining, comical at times, yet very endearing, and attests to the closeness of this tight-knit community.

Sally rates Little Ricky the Boy from Otter Lake 5-STARS

Sally Says: Delightful! Beautiful stories from a more innocent time. I loved this book. It's a beautiful retelling of a childhood experienced and seen through the wonder and awe filled eyes of a delightfully curious little guy called Ricky. It brought back so many memories of my own childhood and genuinely transported me to a more innocent and carefree time. The detail is extraordinary! The writer teases us with mentions of delicious sweets and candy that we all enjoyed as children and had me longing to revisit the sweet shops of my youth! A well written book with obvious love and wonderment bursting out of every page. Buy it to read to your little ones, you'll enjoy it as much as they will.

FIVE BONUS SHORT STORIES
BY AUTHOR RICK J.M. GAUTHIER

- Elementary Years at St. Mary's

- Dad's Dream

- Granny's Humble Furnishings Became the Beginnings of Heirlooms

- The Smallest House in Otter Lake!

- Crafting the 12 Days of Christmas

The five original short stories in this section by author Rick J.M. Gauthier are being included for your reading enjoyment!

Thank you for buying your Little Ricky classic, and in doing so, supporting the author in his efforts to help others.

Elementary Years at St. Mary's - Part I

The year was 1970 and my mother told me that, I, the youngest of her 5 children would now have to start school that autumn, just like my brothers and sister had in years previous. Oh gosh, now it was my turn to go to school! There would be no more watching my TV favourites the "Flintstones" or "Sesame Street" over lunchtime in peace and quiet. There would be no more special time at home with only my Granny and me while my siblings were away at school!

Hence, when that early September 1970 day arrived, after the Labour Day long weekend, I was nudged out the door with my lunch box in hand to go out to the street to wait for the school bus. Even though we lived only about a 10 minute walk from the school, we were mandated to take the bus to school, because Martineau Street in Otter Lake, Quebec was a highway and way too dangerous for little ones to walk along it. So, that morning, Mr. Laprise a wonderful gentleman who lived outside the town drove up with the little yellow school bus and I climbed aboard.

A few minutes later, after turning off Martineau Street, Mr. Laprise drove up and onto the semicircular paved drive of the school yard. He stopped directly in front of the doors of a massive red brick building that was St. Mary's Elementary School. I slowly descended the bus in shock and awe, completely amazed that nearly every child in Otter Lake was assembled here on the

school grounds. I saw many kids I knew and that helped ease my fear of going inside this massive building and starting my "grade 1" studies that morning. We were allowed a little bit of catch-up time to chat with our fellow school mates, and I took the time to take in the surroundings at the front of the school. What amazed me the most was the tall statue on its cement pedestal of Christ the Sacred Heart with its arms raised to Heaven! Surely, I thought to myself, this was a good sign! I would survive the first day of school. I thought about meeting my very first school teacher, but thought more importantly just then, that this school yard was great, because there were lots of grassy areas for relaxing and play time!

Suddenly, the sound of the bell from its belfry atop the school roof and its clang, clang, clang, ordered us to line up, to get ready to enter the red brick beast. As new students, we were met outside by our first grade teacher, Mrs. Louis Fleury. She had a warm smile, but we knew instantly that there was no fooling around with this lady! I wondered, "could I escape, and go back home?" Nope, it was too late! So, all the new grade one students and I assembled at the smaller of the two entrances to the school. The school had two entrances. The first was this one, the entry to the one-story part of the school. The second entrance was larger, and if someone entered there, they would either go directly down a hallway to a large open space which serviced double-duty as the school's auditorium and its cafeteria, or they would go upstairs to where the older grade 5 and 6 kids had classrooms.

The first entrance were I assembled with the other youngsters is the one with big heavy doors. This entry way led to the area where the first, second, third and fourth grade kids had classrooms in our school. Upon entering as instructed by Mrs. Fleury, "that we were to move slowly and quietly", we passed through the impressive entry hallway. It was scary, but because I was curious and was looking around a lot, I first noticed an enormous statue of, "hmmmm? Was it of Jesus or was it of one of the saints", I pondered? In reality, I think it was a statue of the Sacred Heart. I was amazed at how shiny and clean the beautiful maple or perhaps oak wood floors were! To the right were some washrooms. I noted that both boys and girls washrooms were there on the right. As we moved slowly forward, a little further up in the hallway, we were instructed to turn left and turn down a second very long connecting hallway. This in my mind was the passage of many, many rows of endless classrooms! It seemed to go on and on forever and forever. As we were about to reach Mrs. Fleury's classroom, my thoughts drifted back to the washroom doors that I had seen. I imagined that the boys' room probably had urinals. I felt happy that I now knew where to find the bathrooms, should I ever have to avail myself later that day, but strangely I felt afraid of actually using a urinal! You see, at home we had a full bathroom, but we did not have a urinal. As such, I was not sure what a boy was to do when using a urinal! I assure you that in time, I figured it out! One stands there and finds relief! Who knew these amazing inventions existed in this wonderful world, in this small town of ours!

Mrs. Fleury's classroom was the first classroom on the left at the front of the school. This would be our classroom for the next two years; for both grades 1 and 2, but only if we did well and passed Mrs. Fleury's instructions! If we had not turned left towards Mrs. Fleury's classroom, we were told that if we had turned right at the junction, it would have led us to the interior entrance of the Gray Nuns or the Sisters of St. Mary's Convent. Mrs. Fleury cautioned us to always be respectful to the Sisters and not to bother them with our silly questions and nonsense! Being raised Catholic, I already knew and understood the important and sacred work performed by the Sisters. Some of the

Sisters of St. Mary's, nuns of the Sisters of Charity were teachers and they taught mostly the French speaking children from Otter Lake. The others did community and charitable work for the church and the town.

Mrs. Fleury was my mentor and my teacher for my first two years of primary school. She taught most all English kids from town at one point in history!

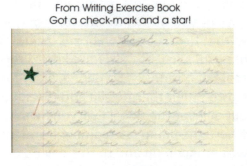

From Writing Exercise Book
Got a check-mark and a star!

I have very fond memories of her teaching us how to form our letters, how to write, how to spell, how to count, and how to add and subtract numbers. As well, there was always time for prayer and song and on several occasions, we performed crafts with the help of another teacher; Mrs. Grace Dale; during those two first years of school.

From Writing Exercise Book - Grade 1

If we behaved well, both in and out of class, and performed well in our studies, we would often be awarded with a 'star' sticker placed in our note books or on special occasions, if a student was very good and worked well in his or her school work, Mrs. Fleury would unlock her storage cupboard and take out the magic container of pink peppermints!

One of the funniest memories I have from these first days of school was the mystery of the leaky lunch box! At that time, our lunch boxes including our thermoses of soup, juice, or milk were kept directly behind the seats of our desks. Someone, and I forget who, did not tighten their thermos lid and the soup or juice leaked out all over the floor! Everyone was curious to know where the liquid was coming from! The mystery liquid was mopped up and to this day no one really knows what transpired!

Other happy times as mentioned above, were enabling us, the first graders to be creative with some arts and crafts during school time. Two of the crafting events

that come to mind now, and are fondly remembered are when we constructed gifts for our mothers to be given to our respective Mom's on Mother's Day. We had glued a full paper plate and a half paper plate together to form a keep-sake kind of paper basket. We then covered these baskets with paper flowers, cut-outs, or string and sometimes painted them to make them more personalized for our mothers. We were then instructed to make Mother's Day cards, with customized messages for our Moms. What a success Mother's Day was that year!

At Christmastime, we created beautiful Nativity figures to decorate our classroom. Mrs. Grace Dale came to our class once again to spend time with us to create two displays of the first Christmas. One was made to resemble stained-glass windows! For this first one, all the characters of the Nativity were formed with cut-out pieces of cardboard, and the cut-outs were then filled in with varied colored tissue paper to make the finished figures look like paper versions of stained glass windows. The cardboard pieces were trimmed to form images of Mary, Joseph, baby Jesus, an angel, some shepherds, stable animals, the Three Wise Men, and even a camel! These figures were then carefully cut to form geometric areas for our paper stained glass pieces to be glued into. The cardboard formed the framing and the tissue paper was our beautiful stained glass pieces. The other set of Nativity characters was formed by completely covering the images of the Manger in tiny paper bow ties made of colored crate paper. These tiny bows were glued to the cardboard cut-outs of the Nativity characters. Blues were reserved for the Virgin Mary, brown and green for St. Joseph, white and yellow for Baby Jesus, etc. These Nativity sets held prominent placement in our classroom windows throughout the Christmas season.

Successfully after two wonderful years under Mrs. Fleury's tutelage, we the grade two pupils graduated to grade 3. As grade three students we had to move

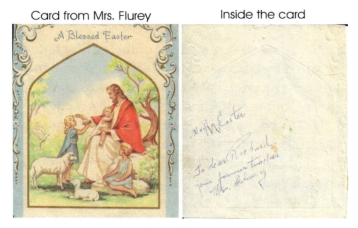

Card from Mrs. Flurey   Inside the card

across the hall to a new classroom at the back of the school. For the next school year, we had to join the new grade 4 students who had just graduated from grade 3. To clarify, in the 1970s in our little Town of Otter Lake, two school grades were taught by one teacher in the same classroom. Grades one and two were always together. Grades three and four were always together, and grades five and six were always grouped together. For now however, with successful completion of both grades one and two my future school year of 1972-73 was yet to come, but first summer break!

Elementary Years at St. Mary's

Elementary Years at St. Mary's - Part II

By now, after having had two previous years' experience at St. Mary's, myself and the other seasoned school kids knew all the routines at the school! We knew the ins-and-outs of school life, the building, the school yard, and all the fun places to

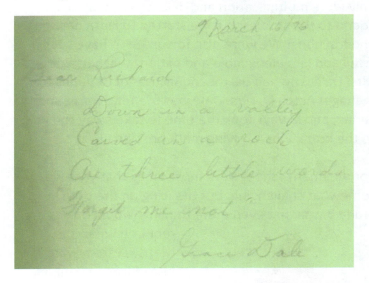

study, play, and hide! Of course, the very best place to hide was the magical janitor's closet! It was a tiny cupboard were the school bell rope hung in secret. This space was indeed one of these special hiding places! In September 1972, I started my grade 3 studies in Mrs. Grace Dale's class. It was a bit scary at first, because we left behind some of our younger former classmates in Mrs. Fleury's classroom and now joined the much more mature older group of the current school year's grade 4 students in this novel environment.

Our studies continued, and the lessons got more difficult. We studied many things, but I mostly remember enhanced reading, and writing, as well as arithmetic or as I called it "Oh gosh - more MATH"! Not only were multiplication and division calculations added to the studies, but we started to learn decimals and fractions! We were also fortunate to have such a swell and knowledgeable and patient teacher! Poor Mrs. Dale who had us, the inquisitive lot of pupils to manage! Actually, Mrs. Dale was friendly, warm and caring, and always took the time to take away the pain to the brain, when solving math problems!

For me, math school work most times that year was somewhat challenging, but the icing on the cake in grade 3 was that even more thinking would be  required when the Metric System was introduced in Canada, all across the country! Previously, in Canada, we all used the Imperial System just like the folks in England. Before any of us had started any formal schooling, the majority of us knew that a foot had 12 inches, a yard had 3 feet, 1 cup was 8 oz, 10 miles was a long way to go, 90 degrees in the shade was hot, 32 degrees would freeze water and your toes, and a pound of fat was a heavy pound of fat! Well, in the early 1970s Canada decided to adopt the Metric System and as such, we had a brand new curriculum to learn. This curriculum was implemented to help each of us best understand the distances, lengths, weights, masses, volumes and temperatures of the future! As such, we got our introduction to the Metric System in 1973 and 1974 at Saint Mary's! In reality, most of us easily learned and adopted the Metric System. It was fairly simple, as we all soon would understand that 1 millimetre times 10 was a centimetre. Ten centimetres times 10 was a decimetre, 10 decimetres times 10 made a hectometre, and 10 hectometres times 10 was 1 kilometre! Wow! Tens, tens, tens across the board! It was the same for volume or litres (and its derivatives) and the same for weight or kilograms (and its derivatives)! Temperatures as well were easy to understand with the Celsius temperature scale of the Metric System in comparison to the older Imperial Fahrenheit System. In the old days temperatures had to be memorized because most were not standard. With Celsius we soon learned, that it was fairly easy, because it was easy to remember that 0 degrees was the freezing point for water and 100 degrees was its boiling point…..Simple right??!!!! Anyhow, we were very fortunate to have once again, our teacher and mentor Mrs. Grace Dale at our side. She was always there to help us assimilate the new and fun Metric System. I remember her arriving to class with a variety of measurement tools, whether they were for weight, volume, temperature or distance, and she would happily demonstrate to us the meaning of the measurements! Mrs. Dale and her well-thought-out learning techniques helped each of us in grade 3 or grade 4 to easily adopt the new Metric System. It was all easy, easy, easy, but now it was time for us to teach our parents and to convince them that the Metric System was the future for everyone!!! Well……we did our best!!!!

In addition to math and metric, we continued to have arts and crafts, and even some history and geography lessons were learned. It was in the third grade, that we had studied the map of Canada, learned the names of all 10 provinces and most big city names of those provinces; well at least the capital city names! To help us with this learning, at the front of our classroom above the huge chalk board was a window blind type, roll-up map contraption. When pulled down into place, it displayed a most beautiful coloured map of Canada. I remember each province and each territory having such vibrant colours. There was shading as well to show elevations like the Rocky Mountains and the Laurentian Shield! Beautiful hues of blue were used to show off the oceans that surrounded Canada. Just looking at this map and talking about the varied places in our country made each young student dream about perhaps visiting these places one day! I fortunately got to visit most of Canada's provinces and territories later on in life as a public servant supporting the Team Canada network.

Everyday life at school, like before, had its daily routine. We started morning class, had our a.m. recess outside, then more class time, then lunch in the auditorium, followed by afternoon class, then our p.m. recess break, and finally the last bit of late afternoon class time before the bell rang to tell us to prepare ourselves for the bus ride or walk home. My favourite time of course while being in grade 3 was recess time!! We were allowed to go outside and play in the school yard, which was a nice break from sitting in class! The girls usually played skipping rope games, girly ball games together, or giggled in groups because they like this boy to that! The boys played baseball, wrestled, or played pirates or pioneer explorers of the lost fort adventures, when we would slide under and hide inside the wooden framed box of the Sisters of St. Mary's huge clothes-stand, which was at the back of the school. The pressure was on, especially when we had to remain absolutely silent, if one of the nuns was actually up there hanging their clothes to the line, and especially when the school bell rang calling us to return to class! Yikes, what to do, get caught by Sister Mary Marthe and get into BIG trouble, or get scolded by Mrs. Dale in class?! Boys will be boys!

Elementary Years at St. Mary's

Elementary Years at St. Mary's - Part III

1974 brought changes to St. Mary's Elementary School and our grade 4 class. Earlier in that school year, our teacher Mrs. Dale had an accident. She had broken her leg and would not be returning to school. Because this happened so long ago, I can't say with 100 percent certainty what type of accident Mrs. Dale actually had, but I do think that she broke her leg in an accident during a Carnival snowmobile race. Of course, we were all concerned for Mrs. Dale, but we also all wondered "Oh oh, we would have a new teacher, but the question was who?" We did get a new teacher, and as well a move to one of the mysterious upstairs classrooms where only the older grades could go!! Our new teacher started soon afterwards and she was instantly loved by her students. Mrs. Paul Blaskie was hired to teach us for the remainder of the year. She was a super great teacher, and was lovingly known to her students as Mrs. "T" based upon the letter the first letter in her given name of Theresa. She was our beloved Mrs. Theresa Blaskie.

Grade 4 studies, as expected intensified. This was no worry, because time spent in class was a lot of fun. The good times happened, because we had a whole new group of students, the former grade two pupils join us as the new grade-three gang. This pairing of the two groups of students made for a year filled with lots of study and lots of adventure. Mrs. Blaskie spent her days teaching us the required curriculum of reading, writing, geography and math; now including long division, and we all did pretty well under her watchful eyes. I have happy memories of her also playing a piano that was in our classroom. This was a great time for music and song. Mrs. Blaskie was also a great story teller. We loved her history lessons.

One of the more bizarre memories from grade 4 that I remember well is when I was no longer so shy and started to be more of a practical joker. Catching one of my younger grade 3 class mates alone in class one day over lunch break, I told her I was going to teach her a trick. She was game, so I said why not? First, I told her to go over to the open window of the classroom, take both index fingers and put them into the sides of her mouth from the inside. Next, I then told her to stretch her cheeks slightly using her fingers within her mouth, and then to shout out the word "puck", as in hockey puck! She was so happy to oblige, and the result was so funny, that I tumbled laughing. You see, the word did not come out as "puck" with a stretched mouth. It sounded more like a not so nice word. Oh well, for a stupid kid, a practical joker, I thought it was pretty funny, until we got caught by a teacher and the school principal. It seemed that some teachers were walking just outside the bank of windows when I had my fellow pupil scream this word loudly out for all to hear. Now, I knew what it felt like to "get the ruler". I deserved it!

That year was also a time when we celebrated winter Carnival at school! If you grew up in Quebec, you knew all about Carnival! All children across the province knew about and looked forward to winter Carnival each February! Carnival time was a fun period for kids and adults alike to celebrate winter. Carnival was filled with activities like: the building and judging of snow

sculptures; pancake breakfasts; dances; sports events; parades; and of course Monsieur Bonhomme Carnaval himself! This particular year, we held a talent show at St. Mary's Elementary School as part of the festivities. This fun event was set up so that a few school children, who would be nominated by their peers, could win the contest and be crowned Carnival King or Carnival Queen! Oh what fun!! I was one of the lucky boys to be nominated to be Carnival King. So with help from my mother to make me a costume, and support and coaching from Mrs. Blaskie, I was to perform as the Singing Cowboy! My mother, who was an excellent seamstress planned out and sewed a wonderful blue cowboy shirt with red fringes for me. Equally, she said that if I took very good care of it, I could borrow my father's big white cowboy hat! Great, now that I had a cowboy look, what would I do for the talent portion of the contest? After  consulting with my grandmother, she thought I could sing well, so I selected a funny jingle I knew and started to practice it! My rendition of Poncho the shooting cowboy, sung to the tune of 'Rudolph the Red Nosed Reindeer' was now set to be my grand act! Of course, please understand that the 1970s was a very different time and kids would be kids. It was a time just after the 1960s, when western television shows were still all the rage and cowboys were king. Today, this tune, similar to many of the cartoons we watched as children are no longer appropriate, especially for children. Thankfully most of us now have a much better understanding of the world and world issues. None-the-less for memory's sake the first part of the tune went like this: "Poncho the shooting cowboy had a very shiny gun. If you ever saw it, you'd just turn and run. All of the other cowboys used to laugh and call him names. They never let poor Poncho play any cowboy games......."! The rest of the song is lost to fade away in history!

My fellow competitors performed other talents more amazing than mine. I remember singers, step dancers, poetry readers, and acting skits. I know for sure, that it was not I who won the contest. My singing needed much more fine tuning to be of any quality. I am still working at it today, but without much success! I do believe it was one of my most cherished classmates, cherished elementary school friends, who won due to her outstanding fast footed step dancing. She was crowned Carnival Queen and we all bowed to her Royal Highness and celebrated her amazing win!

Elementary Years at St. Mary's

Elementary Years at St. Mary's - Part IV

School years 1975-76 and 1976-77 would be the last two elementary years for me and the other children my age. Most of us by 1977 would have been eleven or twelve years old, and it was time for us to leave elementary school. However though high school was on the horizon, we had had the privilege of going to school in our own town at St. Mary's. Later, studies at Secondary School would be in Shawville Quebec. That is the way schooling unfolded for all of the Pontiac Communities in those days and for most it is the same today. When starting elementary school back in 1970, there was a fair group of kids starting with me in grade 1. Over the years, we dwindled down to just 5 students in our grade level. Our grade 5 and grade 6 groups were comprised of only 5, three girls and two boys. Suddenly when one of our buddies moved out to North Western Ontario, we were just 4 from Otter Lake who graduated together at the end of our elementary school studies!

Grade 5 and grade 6 activities, teaching, lessons, and support were provided to us primarily by a very seasoned, professional, and delightful teacher who was the amazing Mrs. Leona Corriveau. Mrs. Corriveau had been a teacher at St. Mary's for many years and was well respected and loved by her students. She was known as the leader in the upstairs "classroom at the back"! For these grades we moved from our upstairs grade 4 classroom down the hall to the end, and into

the prized "classroom at the back"!! Both grade 5 and 6 grade studies involved the usual required reading, writing, math, science, history, and ecology subject lessons with the increased challenges required for each respective grade. I have good memories of having to read out loud to the class and having to write poems and short stories under the critical editor's eye review of Mrs. Corriveau. She was always there to support and guide us through our studies, and to my memory, because of her and her talents as a teacher, our studies went quickly and easily for both grades 5 and 6. We also had one other teacher for part of our studies in grades 5 and 6. For most of us Anglophone children growing up in an English speaking family, it was now time to ensure that we too, the English kids of Otter Lake, could also understand and speak French. A wonderful gentleman called Monsieur Charles would join us a few times a week to give us French lessons. We learned lots of grammar, and spelling and pronunciation for French words, sayings, and short phrases or stories. This wonderful teacher was very patient with us and supported us on our road to becoming bilingual.

Some of the highlights and funny memories I have of being in the classroom at the back, involved typical childhood behaviors and exploration. On one occasion

during our lunch break, a fellow student and I sneaked back into the school, moved quietly up the stairs without being detected by any of the Sisters or Mme. Cartier the lunch monitor! Sneaking In was a tricky adventure, because one had to pass the teacher's room which was right off the school's entrance to its auditorium at the bottom of the staircase. There were always teachers in that room eating their lunch at noon and there were always nuns surveying the downstairs hallway that joined the entryway to the stairs! Of course, the other option was to sneak in through the auditorium's back door and slink through the cafeteria area, where one could better avoid the teacher's room! Not on this day however, because that back door was locked!! Anyhow, on this day my schoolmate and I were successful in getting upstairs and to the back classroom. We really did not want to make any mischief. We just wanted to explore the book and supply closet, and rearrange its contents to help Mrs. Corriveau keep things organized. Instead we spotted her pack of cigarettes on the desk and matches to light one up as well. Yes, back in those days, some teachers smoked, and cigarettes could be left without issue! We all know better today! Well, what would two curious kids do? We decided to sneak one and try it. To avoid detection from a smoked up classroom, we intelligently opened up a window, took one cigarette out of the pack, and while hanging our heads outside, lit it up! We coughed and sputtered and felt ill. To make things worse for me, the confounded cigarette tasted mint, because they were menthol! I hated mint! At that time, I despised mint. Now that the cigarette was lit, we were not sure what to do with it? How would we dispose of a lit cigarette without anyone finding it? Well the only thing to do of course, was to finish smoking it!! Upon finishing it, we threw the smudged-out butt out the window. We had hoped we would go and bury it in the sand later that day. We then swished the smoke as much as we could, out the windows and I do believe that we did not get caught! Well that is how I remember it! I am sure however, due to her eagle eye glances at me all that afternoon, Mrs. Corriveau knew!

Throughout all six grades of our elementary school year education, some sort of physical activity was always encouraged by the teachers. Definitely there were always two outdoor recess breaks; both morning and afternoon, and at least 30 to 40 minutes of being outdoors each day after having eaten our lunches. Our lunches were eaten sitting at two rows of long tables in the cafeteria. Once we swallowed down our food and cleaned up the tables, off we would go to play outside. Often the younger kids would gather naturally, to play games of tag, or hide and seek, or hop scotch. The girls would partake in skipping rope and the boys would play ball games. Like mentioned in Part III above, some boys would bring their "Hot Wheels" toy cars to school and all young lads and some of the girls would gather around to play with our tiny cars racing them quickly down the little roads we made in the sand at the back of the school.

In both grades 5 and 6, more formal physical education was introduced to us. A physical education teacher, Mr. Pierre was hired to help us be more active and to introduce us to the rules of popular sports like hockey, basketball, baseball and soccer. I believe he was an athlete, but I cannot remember this detail accurately,

however he was muscularly fit and could have been an athlete! I know though that he was instrumental in making sure our little school in Otter Lake could partake in and enjoy the World Olympics as much as any other Canadian or world citizen would. The year was 1976 and Montreal, Quebec was the place to be in order to see, with one's own eyes, the spectacular games called the Olympics. Mr. Pierre understood that most of us at St. Mary's, could only dream of a trip to Montreal, so he instead worked with the other teachers to hold our very own Olympic Games! Mr. Pierre taught us all about summer Olympic sports like the high jump, the shot put, the javelin, the disks, the 25 metre race, the long jump, the hurtles, etc. We learned excitedly about the origins of the Olympic Games and the significance of the Olympic rings. On the day of our mock-Olympics, there were no classes that day! Yeah, screamed all the kids! We spent one whole day outside competing in these Olympic events and we all

proudly applauded our winners at our very own gold, silver, and bronze medal ceremony. How well did I do, you may ask at our little Olympic Games? Sadly, there was no medal for 4th, 5th, 6th, or 7th place, so as a result my feet never left the ground to climb the podium, nor did any medal adorn my neck!

Well, that is the end of this story. I completed my elementary school years at the beginning of the summer of 1977 and said good-by for the final time to St. Mary's Elementary School. The next chapter of life would be high school or as it is called in Quebec, Secondary School. We knew already that our studies would continue in Shawville, Quebec at Victoria Avenue High School or VAHS, but not yet, first summer break!!

Dad's Dream

Our father Cyril Gauthier, a long time resident of Otter Lake, Quebec, was one of the many small business owners in our town. From the earliest memories of my youth, until his tragic passing from cancer in spring of 1986, I remember Dad working hard day and night in his shop, always ready to help customers 7 days a week. Dad, a very experienced mechanic, used his technical skills and the town's need for small engine repair work, to start his very own small business; a business that grew over the years to develop into what I mostly remember as Gauthier and Son's Garage of Otter Lake, Quebec. This small business was one of our father's most well-known and cherished legacies.

Previous to starting his own business, our father honed his skills and know-how of fixing things from his early days of living with his mother and siblings at their homestead along Sandy Creek, in and around a humble home they had way up on the Picanoc Road. Our grandmother Gertrude Gauthier was a young widow and as such, relied upon her children to help keep their home in good repair while she worked where she could to earn enough to support her young family. I assume that because of the times, she relied mostly upon her boys, my father and my Uncle Eddie Gauthier, to maintain and repair the bigger things. Of course, this is not to say that Dad's sisters Gladys and Beatrice did not do their share! All four children worked hard, worked lovingly to support their mother.

Later in life, Dad found more formal work as a mechanic in Renfrew Ontario and again in Ottawa after that. He worked at a few motor garages in both cities and used these opportunities not only to provide for his family, but also to further hone his skills as a competent mechanic.

At one point in the late 1950s or around 1960, our father and his young family made the move back to Dad's beloved Otter Lake. Mother and Father made Otter Lake their home until their respective deaths. Mother and Father purchased property, and shortly after that Dad set up his small engine business in what we referred to lovingly as the "Old Shop or the Old Garage". It is in this first building, that I can vividly remember my father working away every day on the repair of every type of small engine imaginable that townsfolk brought to him in a broken-down or non functioning condition. Dad's clients included town residents, nearby towns' residents, and bushmen from all over the Pontiac, all needing chainsaws, pumps, lawnmowers, garden tillers, or any other mechanical device repaired. There were also tourists and local sport fishers needing fixing of their out-board motors which they needed in order to drive their fishing boats. In wintertime of course, these same folks would support Dad in the big business of snowmobile repairs! Winter was the time when attention was needed to keep these winter vehicles in good repair. Snowmobiling was all the rage in those days and who could survive a long winter without a snowmobile ride?! Our father did work on motor vehicles like trucks and cars from time-to-time, but his specialty was small engine repair.

The Old Shop was an A-framed wooden building that featured two large swinging doors at its front, a cement ramp for easier entry at the foot of these

doors, a steep asphalt shingled roof, wooden gables, a side main entry door, and old fashioned glass pained windows, which permitted ample daylight to enter. The edifice's walls were nearly completely covered in the same faux brick gray/black asphalt siding, which was the same siding that adorned our house. The building had a huge storage loft in its attic. A wooden staircase was hidden in between two of the shop's ceiling joists and it could be lowered and lifted by way of a pulley system. The secret rope that worked the magic pulley, to permit access to the loft was hidden away from the kids so that we would not stray up to dangerous and spooky spaces!

More space was made available in a wooden addition at the back of the shop. I can remember this space being stuffed with rows and rows of outboard motors, all clamped securely to large planks of wood that were attached to the walls.

Along the interior of the main shop, one would find large work benches, of which sat a variety of machinery or devices, such as vices, grinders, saws, testers, etc. Above and below the benches were Dad's pride and joy, his tools. A variety of tool chests were strategically placed to give Dad easy access to the tool he needed, at the time when he needed it. Dad's rule was every tool has its place and once used, it had to be returned to its place. Rule two was to not break rule one. I never broke Dad's rules! Well maybe once!

This first official structure that became Gauthier's Garage was powered by electricity through an underground cable that came from the house. The main area, rear area and loft above, were lit by plain electric light bulbs that hung from the ceiling or were mounted above the work areas. Electrical outlets were strategically placed above the workbenches, which easily permitted the powering of any electrical drills, sanders, testers, or other such tools. However, the coolest device within Dad's garage, in my view was the intercom system! This novel system permitted calls to- and-from the house. A long copper wire ran between the house's kitchen window, across the yard, and directly to the roof gable of the shop. Each end of this wire was connected to mini plastic battery operated phones. Imagine that two D-cell batteries tucked inside each phone module allowed instant communication!

We must all remember that back in the 1960s or 1970s, cell phones did not exist! For that matter, most homes did not even have a telephone or if they did, the home was on a party line! This intercom system was used when Dad needed to speak with our mother about a part order, the whereabouts of a stock item, or to summon her to the shop to write up an invoice. Sometimes he just used it to tell our mother that he loved her! These phones were also most importantly used by us his kids, to tell Dad when meals were hot and ready at both dinnertime and suppertime.

Over the years, Dad's business grew, and as such, so did his need for more space. More space was becoming even more important, because my older brothers were growing up and slowly each would be taking on their respective roles as apprentice mechanics. Each of them decided to join the family business and work alongside our father at Gauthier's Garage. In the mid-1970s, our father hired a few carpenters to work with him to design and construct the new cement block building. In no time at all, a cement foundation was poured. On this solid foundation, the cement block walls slowly started to rise higher and higher. A large opening at the front was planned so that this space could be transformed into a huge roller windowed garage door! This space was made large enough to bring in bigger cars, trucks or large motors for repair. Along the same frontage as the big rolling door, the primary entry door and one large window at the building's corner were also planned. It was decided that the side wall facing the street and the back wall of the building would include spaces for one large single window respectively. The side facing the "Old Shop" would include a side door.

Once the walls were completed, the roof trusses, the plywood sheathing, and the aluminum roofing sheets were raised and put into place. Now that the new

home for Gauthier's Garage had a finished roof, the cement for a smooth durable floor was mixed and poured. Lastly, to complete the exterior, the window and door frames were finished, which enabled their respective doors and windows to be put into their proper places. Within days, the interior spaces were now being tackled. The ceiling went up and the building's electrical and heating systems were installed. This time, a new hydro hook-up was used to bring electricity into the building directly and as such a brand new breaker box was hooked-up at the front entrance. The heating system chosen was an oil forced air furnace, which was placed at the back of the shop. A large heating duct ran along the ceiling from the back to the front and smaller pipes branched off of it to bring heat to all areas of the garage. Later with the rising price of oil, Dad also installed a big wood burning furnace in a more central area of the shop. So, unless the big door was left open everyone was warm and toasty inside. Sometimes, when the wood furnace was stocked and burning furiously, one would feel the heat of summer! How did the temperature get controlled? If it got too hot inside, Dad would simply open the door!!!

Once the new work benches were built and installed, the tools from the old garage were moved to the new garage and strategically placed in their new home. A customer service desk was built and installed at the rear making it an official place for our mother to greet customers and to manage all the stock catalogs and paper work. In this same location, my brother Chris also set up his budding side business of selling soda pop and salty or savory snacks. He installed in this spot a Coca Cola cooler and Hostess Chip rack. This same year, our father was also expanding the types of mechanical work he and my brothers would be doing, so Dad had purchased and installed a new electric welder, a bigger air compressor, a large chain hoist that hung from the ceiling, which was a device for lifting heavy motors, a new grinder, two heavy duty vices, and a huge new lathe. The lathe was an amazing tool which enabled Dad to actually fashion most parts he needed, especially those that did not exist! Dad showed a great sense of invention and ingenuity!

The final addition during this time was the appendage of a wooden walkway built between the two buildings. The side window of the old garage structure was removed and an open doorway was put into its place. A small bridge connecting the side doorway of the new cement block building and the new opening to the old garage was constructed. On this bridge, two side walls went up and a peaked roof was added atop which totally enclosed the space. This new walkway or passageway became the home for the gas and oil can storage, but its primary purpose was to permit easy access between the new garage and the old. With this new passageway, Dad or my brothers no longer needed to face rain or snow to enter the "Old Shop"! The old garage remained an integral part of the business and did not become a forgotten space. It was now mostly used for storage of used, but very valuable stock, motors, and parts. On several occasions, this storage depot was the only place to find a unique part!

After several good years of increased business and continued hard work, our father decided to expand his business once again. Over time as Dad worked in his trade, he had become an authorized dealer for several small engines and products such as: Evinrude; Ski-doo; Meyers; Johnson; Lawnboy; Roper; Briggs and Stratton;

Dad's Dream

and Jonsered. With so many new wares to sell, he now needed more space to showcase them. When I close my eyes, I can vividly remember the variety of small engines, boats, and motors that were sold at Gauthier's Garage. These included snowmobiles, outboard motors, tillers, chainsaws, lawnmowers, pumps, and aluminum boats, just to name a few of the ones that I can recollect and are etched in my mine. So once again, the planning started to add two additions to the cement block structure of our father's garage. For the first, Dad envisioned a long open space to be adjoined to the left side of the garage, the side that ran parallel to Martineau Street. This new space was to be the official "Showroom", a space to display the shiny new items for sale. The second addition in Dad's expansion plan was to construct a long narrow room at the back of the existing garage. This new space would become our mother's new stockroom and office.

Both additions were once again built using cement block construction. The blocks were laid on the new cement foundations which were framed and poured to the left and at the rear of the garage. Soon, the new walls were completed. Atop the new walls, adapted trusses were fashioned and adjoined to the existing garage roof. On these trusses, new plywood sheathing and aluminum roofing panels were nailed into place. Smooth new cement floors were poured in both areas. A traditional car garage door was framed and installed at the front of the showroom. This entrance would enable prospective customers to enter and browse the showroom directly from outside. To brighten both new spaces, large bright and pane-free windows were added; three in the showroom, and one in the back stockroom. To access the new spaces from inside, two of the original exterior garage windows were changed to become doorways. A window at the front of the garage transformed into a set of double doors and the rear window was changed to be the doorway to the office and stockroom.

Lastly, upon our mother's suggestion and vision, the majority of the building was painted in the Evinrude blue, red and white! With our help, Mother brushed

the front and street side walls with bright and clean stripes of fresh white, then red, then blue. She trimmed the windows and doors in a bright new coat of cheery blue. The old brown window and door frames were no longer in fashion! The crowning to finish off all the expansion work however, was the re-installation of the large Evinrude sign and the oversized thermometer, both of which took a prominent place directly under the big halogen light fixture. This bright lamp fully lit the yard during the night due to its perfect high-up location sturdily affixed to the peak of the roof. Now once again, with the signage back in place, everyone who arrived would know that this beautifully enhanced building was indeed the home of "Cyril Gauthier and Sons Garage"! Dad was proud to have his sons working for him, so he insisted that "Sons" be included in the business's name going forward. My contribution to this event was the construction of a wooden miniature model of Gauthier and Son's Garage. I measured the cement block building, including its two new additions and then fashioned a realistic model of it from a sheet of plywood, some balsa wood, heavy duty tin foil, and cellophane plastic sheets. I painted the model using the same paint colours Mom had chosen for the building the model was inspired from. This little garage model was placed on Dad's truck roof and was displayed driving around town for a town celebration parade. It was then displayed for several years in the garage's showroom and office.

Customers would arrive by car or by foot. Folks arriving in their vehicles would park without issue in the large sandy parking area, and then make their way leisurely to greet Dad, Mom, or one of my brothers. Walkers would simply pass the open drive entryway and stroll in right up to the open garage doors. Anyone and everyone arriving were warmly greeted with an inviting smile and a lively "How are you today?" Often during the summer months, patrons could find my brother Bernie standing firmly beside the test water tank validating a repair of yet another outboard motor. This tank was a huge barrel in which outboards could be run without Bernie having to actually go to a lake and take a boat ride to test his repair work! Bernie would often tease any passerby by saying, "Hey the water is nice. Do you want to jump in for a swim?!!" Folks could find my brother Chris, with a torque wrench in hand, ready for him to remove the cutting blade from a lawnmower that he was repairing. They would see that he had just determined that the blade needed sharpening or replacement. Upon noticing the newcomer, Chris would jump up and instantly put out a friendly hand as he would say, "How do you do? What can I do for you today?"

Upon stepping into the shop, customers could find our father hard at work. Dad would be most likely hunched down with his welding helmet on, tacking two pieces of metal together with his new electric welder or bent over one of the workbenches magically making a once defunct engine whirr to life once more! As soon as Dad noticed a new customer arriving, he would instantly get up and greet the person with his cheery, "Well hello, what can we do for you? I am sure we can work something out to fix your problem today." After having a quick look around, the visitor would find my brother Brian working away at a water pump or chainsaw at one of the work benches. Brian would nod, smile and say, "Gidday, How is it going?" Customers would finally find Mom standing at her post behind the customer service desk. She would have a handful of invoices or one of her trusty notebooks in her hand and a pencil behind her ear, because she had been counting parts to update the stock list or was looking after the accounts receivables or payables. Noticing the arrival of a client, Mom would bookmark her note or her invoice and quickly come out from behind the desk, scurry around the wood furnace, and move forward to greet the new visitor. Mom's eyes would twinkle and her sweet smile would end up turning into her verbal smile of a warm "Hello and welcome to Gauthier's".

Once inside the garage, one would find themselves looking down the length of the building to the back and the customer service desk. Directly behind the desk, one would instantly notice Christopher's Coca Cola machine enticing them to perhaps buy a soda?! Beyond the drink machine, one could see the open entry door to the back stockroom and office. Once through the main entry door of the garage, to the left one could see the open doors to the showroom and a glimpse of the new items for sale inside. If one glanced slightly right, a clear view of the electric welder was there. Along the far right wall, an air compressor and the gas welding tank set were in clear view. Further down that wall, the customer would see a doorway.

This secret door was the entryway to the gas and oil storage area and a passage way to enter the "Old Shop". Turning just a bit more to one's right, Dad's lathe was housed against that wall. This big green turning machine was one of Dad's prized possessions. Finally, when looking again further down that side, the back right corner presented the large main workbench, including the iron vice and grinder which were both bolted to it. Lastly, directly across from the workbench, the visitor could appreciate the varied tool chests, stuffed with every type of tool a good mechanic needed. Tucked behind the tool chest one would then find the oil furnace and its oil tank. Their location was the perfect location because they were tucked away at the back.

In wintertime of course, the same members of the family would still be there! They were of course doing something slightly different as they performed their

work during this season. Dad and my brothers were probably working on snowmobiles, snow blowers or any other kind of winter apparatus that ran using a gas small engine! Mother would be out in the shop as well working away in the office or stockroom or stoking the fire in the wood furnace to keep her men warm. My sister Audrey and I had other duties. In the early days, we were too young to work in the garage with the others, because we lacked the mechanical trade skills. Our focus was school and taking care of our grandmother or the housekeeping and the meals. There are times however, when both my sister and I were able to contribute to the family business. At Christmas time, Dad permitted me to decorate the showroom with handmade ornaments and garlands. I was always delighted to put up a small Charlie Brown-like Christmas tree. It was a thrill to adorn each motor for sale in the showroom with a bright red Christmas bow and a "Buy me for Christmas" tag. Audrey's contribution during the festive season was the addition of her amazing design and creation of a life-sized Santa Claus cut-out! Each Christmas season Santa was found in the loft of the "Old Shop", brought outside to the crisp and cold winter day, hoisted up to the roof, and screwed securely to the wall under the eaves at the front of the garage. Throughout the festive season, Audrey's Santa would wave happily to anyone who passed by! In later years, due to Santa's weight gain or age, he got nailed to the entry door!!

Dad's Dream

The memories and imagery described above are snippets of some of the most cherished moments we built together as a family. However, as we can all acknowledge with the passage of time, things do indeed change. Our father, Cyril Gauthier tragically and suddenly died from a short struggle with cancer in the mid-80s. Despite our loss, the business continued for many, many more years under the leadership of my brother Bernard and my mother Veronica. Both Chris and Brian also continued to work in the business as well. My sister and I graduated from school, found work, and each had moved away to build our own respective careers. In 2000, our mother was faced with some serious health issues of her own and she as well too quickly passed away in 2001. After her death, Bernie and Chris soldiered on and kept the business running. Brian had branched out his work interests in a few other directions, but did continue to support our elder brothers to run the business when he could. And finally, with Bernie's retirement and Christopher's continued illness and eventual passing, this meant the family business had now ended. Unofficially, Bernie continued to support some customers, but the business that once was flourishing was no more. In the last few years of his life, Bernie struggled with terminal cancer, and sadly he as well passed away in 2022.

All of this dear reader is the evolution of everything, the beginning, the good, the bad, and the end. I am certain that both you and I can acknowledge that nothing in life will stay the same forever, because time passes and things do indeed change. It is the way and we have no choice but to let life happen. Despite the present state of a once thriving business, nothing but the happiest memories remain. I will cherish these memories forever, and I am sure that other individuals who were there with us for the journey will fondly remember as well. I am indeed very proud of my father's accomplishments and the love and support provided to him by his wife and his children.

I feel certain that a wide range of clients from far and wide would echo my sentiments. After all, without the loyal customers and support from the community, Dad's business would have not succeeded! Our father, our mother, and my brothers used their skills, experience, and knowledge to fulfill a wanted need for such expertise in Otter Lake. I take pride in knowing that Dad's little business helped: the lumberjacks get back to cutting trees with renewed chainsaws; the fishermen and women, and cottagers to once again launch their boats on the lake with the whirr of a fixed outboard; that tourists and cottagers alike, had fresh water because of a now properly functioning water pump; that townsfolk and community had crisp cut green lawns, because of the renewed roar of a sharpened and overhauled lawnmower; that happy homeowners could now snow blow their laneways with the buzz of their fixed snow blowers; and of course those smiling winter enthusiasts yelping with joy as they glide their fully functioning snowmobiles over the bed of crisp cold snow!

Granny's Humble Furnishings Became the Beginnings of Heirlooms

When I was a youngster, I spent a lot of time helping our Granny, Mrs. Gertrude Blaskie-Gauthier with chores around our homestead or outside in her extensive flower and vegetable gardens in Otter Lake, Quebec. As we worked together, she often shared her stories of the old times with me; several of which were related to the importance of taking good care of one's possessions. On several occasions, she told me how she came about owning certain things, their significance to her, and some of their history. Two of these items were her set of wooden table and chairs and her armed sofa and easy chair set. Granny's feeling was that things were acquired for a purpose and were meant to be used. Throughout her life she did indeed use, but equally looked after her possessions. When our grandmother passed away in 1983, her furnishings for the most part were left to my parents. After my father died in 1986, I decided to permanently move to and work in Ottawa. I had completed my Business Intensive Computer Operators Program and was already being offered temporary clerical jobs in Ottawa, making the timing right for a move to the city. As such, I put plans in place to rent my first apartment. At that time, because I would be needing furniture, my mother gifted to me Granny's table and set of five chairs, and her worn, but much loved sofa and armchair set.

From what I remember, I believe that Granny told me that the original set of six chairs was a wedding present to her from her new husband Rheal Gauthier.

According to her, this set of chairs was well used by everyone at the farm homestead where they lived across the Picanoc River at Sandy Creek. During that time, one of the six chairs got broken and was beyond repair; hence only 5 chairs remained. I continue to be unclear if the table was part of the original set, but according to the many stories about the table that were told by Granny; she said that the table was known to her as her "work horse" because meals and just about everything else imaginable were done on this table! Overtime of course, that table became very heavily worn. The wear and tear of its original tabletop can be attributed to the ample times when Gertrude would cut up meats, garden produce, or other foods on the table throughout the seasons, but especially at harvest and the making of preserves times. When the wearing got to a certain beyond saving point, the tabletop had to be replaced. According to the story, it was replaced using old barn boards! These barn boards were cut to the right length, nailed securely into place upon the base and legs, sanded smooth, and covered with a fresh coat of white enamel paint!

As such, the table that I have always known in Granny's front parlour in our homestead could be the original one from Sandy Creek; the one with a barn board top; the table that came with the set of chairs, or perhaps it could be a table that was brought from Ottawa to Otter Lake when our grandmother who worked and lived in Ottawa for a while moved back to Otter Lake to live with us. If this is the case, it would have happened when Gertrude moved back to Otter Lake at the time when her daughter, our Aunt Bea Kavanagh, got married. I do however believe that it must be the original table from Sandy Creek, because its top is definitely not the original one. It does look and feel like the softwood of barn boards, and the nail heads are clearly evident where they were hammered into the tabletop so many years ago!

My memories of the small dinette set are from my days when I was living on Martineau Street in my hometown. The table and chairs were kept mostly in the front parlour of the house, which was considered Granny's part of the house. The set was not normally used for eating, but could have been used as an extension to the big kitchen table when lots of relatives would come for visits and big meals were served. It was mainly used by Granny to play cards or to plan her quilts or to plant her flowers, etc. Because Granny's sitting room was also the TV room, the chairs were often used by my siblings and me when watching TV. While I was living at home in Otter Lake, I remember the set being painted several times and usually the chairs were redone every couple of years in some shade of brown paint. The table legs were painted the same brown and its top was always painted white. At some time in the 1960s or 70s, I do remember the set being painted black and white; which was a new look that my mother Veronica wanted to try.

In the mid-1980s, just before I moved to Ottawa, I took an interest in refinishing furniture. I had stripped the paint from the table and chairs, made repairs to all chair joints, and re-stained everything in a mahogany colour. Of note, I nearly ruined the chairs! I thought it would be much easier to simply cut off their backs with a carpenter's saw to refinish the wood! What a mistake, because I soon discovered that the back rung spindles could not be easily re-attached! Thankfully, a family relative, Mr. Isadore Blaskie, a fine carpenter in his day, was able to fix the set of chairs by making new back chair rungs and by attaching everything once again like new. The set then moved with me to Ottawa when I rented my first apartment on Carling Avenue. From there, I brought them to my other future Ottawa apartments on Richmond Road, Gladstone Avenue, Laurier Avenue, Cooper Street, and then finally to the house I purchased on Hinchey Avenue.

When I was the owner of Granny's set of table and chairs, only minor repairs were required from time-to-time; especially when loose chair rungs had to be re-glued! In October 2018, because I decided to sell the house and downsize to an apartment or condominium, the dinette set made its way from Ottawa back to Otter Lake to be kept in storage for my niece Kayla. Kayla would use the furnishings when she would be ready to set up her first home. Kayla had shown great interest in inheriting her great-grandmother's furniture, and I was pleased that this set would continue to be kept in our immediate family. The table and chair set is now used in Kayla's beautiful dining room.

With respect to Granny's sofa and big armchair, to the best of what I can remember, based on what she told me, is that this sofa set was moved from Ottawa to Otter Lake when my grandmother decided to move back to the country and live with her son Cyril, our mother, my brothers, and my sister. This was the time when Granny left the rooming house that she had managed in the city for quieter times back in Otter Lake, after her daughter, our Aunt Bea, got married. The sofa and armchair set were used by them and their guests when Granny Gauthier and Aunt Bea lived on Booth Street in Ottawa. I am uncertain, but I would expect they got it second hand, because they did not have a lot of money to spend in those days. In its early life, the set was upholstered in lush caramel brown velvet. The couch had three big comfy square cushions. The chair had a matching, but single cushion. The arm fronts and bottoms of both the chair and sofa were trimmed with beautiful decorative wood.

During the period when the set was at our homestead on Martineau Street in Otter Lake, the sofa was used in several places around the house. At first, it was in the

area behind the kitchen, and was placed under the back window that looked out onto the garden. At another time, it was placed in the main kitchen area just below the stairs along the staircase wall which was close to the basement door. Later, when it was getting too worn out, it spent some time in the basement, and finally it was moved and left out year round on the front veranda at our home on Martineau Street. When I close my eyes, I still clearly see family or friends seated on it enjoying conversation, a bite to eat, or a fun television program. When it was out on the front veranda, this is the place where I would often sit with my grandmother when she would share her fascinating stories in the warm afternoons of spring or fall, or in the cool evenings of summer. One story that I vividly remember is the time she recounted over and over again the day when my sister Audrey and I inadvertently locked poor Granny out of the house despite the fact that she was our official "babysitter" that day!

With regard to the big armchair, as far as I can remember, while living in Otter Lake, it was in the front part of our home. This room was often referred to as the parlour or living room. In this room, the big old arm chair was placed just beside the doorway that led to the kitchen. This seat was mostly Dad's chair, because after his long day of work, he would like to relax in this comfortable chair watching the news on television, or spending time with his mother or other family members in daily conversation. This beloved chair had lots of use, and as such was starting to get worn. So, at one point in time, I clearly remember my mother taking great pains to recover it beautifully in a brown, black, and diamond covered fabric. She did an amazing job and made the chair look like new once more. She also reaffixed the large springs in the chair's back with new strong and wide strips of fabric. As she sewed these, she had teased me not to get too close while she stitched with the biggest needle I had ever seen!

She cautioned me that if I came closer, she would have to give me additional booster shots in my arm! Ouch! I stayed away! At a later time, to help keep the newly recovered chair clean from the oils and grease that made their way in from Dad's garage, Mother made and strapped beautiful mint greenish blue arm and back covers to it. These handy covers were made of a leatherette fabric, making them easy to wipe away any grime. She also made a similar cover for the cushions of our grandmother's rocking chair and these changes dramatically brightened the room.

In the early days, quick fixes to refurbish the wear and tear to the couch included simply covering the sofa with a blanket on the seat and back, and putting matching towels over its arms. After all, as far as we were concerned, it was comfort that mattered most. When the couch became too worn out to simply cover it with a blanket, our mother re-covered it with a strong canvas fabric and then painted this cloth with a dark brown paint to imitate rich brown leather! The armchair had also been spruced up many times with store bought slipcovers from Sears, Stedman's, Zellers, or Giant Tiger. Both chair and couch used to have huge seat cushions. I remember these well, because I used to use the three sofa cushions and the chair cushion to build a small fort in the living area to hide! Those cushions sure did make great building blocks for a prince's castle! What children will do to have fun! Unfortunately, all of these cushions were lost or damaged over the years and thrown away.

When I moved to Ottawa and into my first apartment on Carling Avenue, my mother gave the set to me. The sofa was loaded on my brother Bernie's truck from the

Granny's Humble Furnishings Became the Beginnings of Heirlooms

front veranda, and the chair was brought up from the basement where it was being stored and loaded as well. Once loaded, the sofa and big armchair made their way back to the city from which they originated. By this time, because of much usage and love of this set over the years, sadly both sofa and chair were in quite a tattered shape. However, because I had no furniture, I made use of them none-the-less and simply covered them with new warm blankets to give each piece of the set an almost new look! Eventually, after finding steady employment and saving enough money, I decided to reupholster the set. I completely stripped the sofa and chair down to their wooden bones and steel springs, then rebuilt and recovered each in a similar fabric to what the original velvet fabric had been. This time however, the fabric was not caramel brown, but burgundy. Because all of the seat cushions had been lost to time, I used one large piece of high density foam for the couch seat and another smaller piece for the chair seat. I felt this change made a remarkable improvement, because the set now mimicked a more Victorian look! However, this also meant no more princes' castles! I had grown too big to play in cushion forts in any regard!!

This refurbishment served me well over many years and, I actively used the beautiful furniture in all of my many apartments in Ottawa. However, when I moved to my place on Cooper Street where I had one wall of large sunny windows in my apartment, the hot sun completely ruined the fabric. With little money to buy a new couch to replace this one, I decided to reupholster the set once again! This time though, it was redone in a burgundy rose floral pattern fabric – something I had found at a clearance sale. This recovering unfortunately only lasted a few years, because the fabric was not durable enough for upholstery use. Who knew?! It seemed that I still had a lot to learn about suitable fabrics for upholstery! Oh well, I thought it was still a very comfortable couch and chair. However, when it started to fade and fray badly, I had to do something one more time! After only two summers of facing the bright sunny windows, the sun finally ruined this new fabric completely. For a temporary fix, I made burgundy slipcovers from a bed sheet set. These slipcovers still exist today and do make excellent dust covers! I did not completely like the set's look under the slipcovers I made, because it made the set look like something that would be in the parlour of an old 50s television show!! They did have to do though, until yet another redo job could be managed! They are now a bit faded, but do help protect the set when it is not being used.

So, the beloved living room set continued to be used for another few years, new slipcovers and all. However, in time, I knew I really wanted to recover the furniture yet once more! I felt the set deserved to have at least one more reincarnation. Hence, in the mid-90s on a shopping trip to Montreal, a big city where there are dozens and dozens of fabric stores, I purchased some excellent and sturdy diamond shaped burgundy upholstery fabric and got excited to re-do the set. It took several weeks, but with hard work I completely reupholstered both the sofa and big chair for the last time, enhancing them to their current "looking-like-new state". When I moved to my home on Hinchey Avenue, the set became the focal point of the front parlour directly off the formal entry hallway of the house for the next 21 years.

In the fall of 2018 because of a back injury, and my inability to continue to maintain the house and yard fully, I decided to sell the house and downsize to a much smaller apartment or condominium. I knew that a downsizing meant smaller spaces and as such, it was time to let some pieces of furniture go. I knew I would not have enough space for everything in a much smaller home. Therefore, in the fall of 2018, Granny Gauthier's much loved sofa and armchair set was transported back to Otter Lake and put into storage and safe keeping for my niece. Some years earlier, Kayla had expressed interest in inheriting the set and proudly using both armchair and couch in her own first home.

In recent years, Kayla took huge steps on the route to adulthood and independence when she rented herself at first an apartment, and now a house! After taking occupancy of these new spaces, she had her table and chairs, and her sofa and armchair set moved in. She proudly sets out and uses these treasured family heirlooms. I am thrilled that I was able to pass along her great-grandmother's possessions to her, to continue the evolution of the transfer of family heirlooms from one generation to the next. I know my niece Kayla to be very intelligent, imaginative, hardworking, and an inventive young lady, so I do believe she will take good care of these loved possessions, just as her Great-grandmother Gertrude, Grandmother Veronica, and Uncle Rick did. I hope she has many, many, many happy years of using these prized possessions throughout her life and will now build her own special memories sitting around that table with family or friends or lounging on that burgundy sofa and big old armchair while relaxing after a full day of work or fun. Perhaps she, in time, will keep the evolution going, by passing these treasures on to her own children, her sister, her cousins, or other close family relatives.

I am positive that our Granny, Gertrude Gauthier, a gentle soul but strong-willed lady who first acquired these things, would be so very proud.

The Smallest House in Otter Lake!

Where was the smallest house in Otter Lake situated? How small was it? Who built it? Who lived there? What is its history? Where is it today? These are all good questions, and all will be revealed below!

The year was 1982 and it was the beginning of the summer. I left school that year with two goals in mind. First, I wanted to investigate my loves of architecture and model building and second, I wanted to use my creativity exploring these two venues to craft a special gift for my parents. As they would be celebrating their 29th wedding anniversary at the end of summer in early September, I knew I had plenty of time to make them something memorable for their special day. Mom and Dad were married over the September Labour Day weekend in 1953. As such, my mother would quip that since getting married on Labour Day, they had laboured every day since! They were both indeed hard workers and did labour most days, but not every single day; especially Sundays, despite mother's ongoing joke! Dad worked tirelessly in his small engines shop with Mom by his side as his trusted bookkeeper. When not tending to the books, mother also worked to keep house and in her vegetable gardens. Dad in addition to working in his shop to provide for the family, worked to maintain the house to keep it in good repair. Anniversaries and birthdays for our family were important to each of us, and we always took the time to acknowledge and celebrate such milestones.

This particular year, as mentioned above, my dream was to build for my parents, a scale model of their home, a place they loved and worked hard to make safe and comfortable for each of us; for themselves, their five children, and our grandmother. My first important task was to measure and understand the true scale of our house. As such, out came our 24 foot ladder, the longest measuring tape I could find, and my trusty note book! Everything, absolutely everything got measured and noted. Whether, it was walls, roofs, gables, floors, windows, doors, steps, veranda, wood shed, etc., everything was measured precisely in feet to the nearest inch. Everything inside as well needed to be sized up and this included the interior walls, staircase, rooms, floors, ceilings, doorways, cupboards, furnishings and appliances! Each item or location in and out of the house was measured and noted in my faithful notebook! Next, after studying my notes came the time to draw sketches and to layout the steps I would take to start construction. In my view, the next logical step was to make a decision on what building materials to use. Both stiff and light cardboard, tissue paper, and clear cellophane plastic were chosen to be the primary materials to assemble the model house. Additionally, wallpaper scraps, leftover flooring tiles, and a brown wood stain were chosen to add to the supplies I would need to make this little house eventually look as realistic and life-like as possible.

So, how does one start to build a scale model of one's parent's home? It starts with converting all previous measurements to a smaller scale. I chose that for each foot measured, a one centimeter equivalent would be used. With this in mind, I started drawing out the exterior house walls and roof pieces on light cardboard. After having sketched the four primary walls, I carefully measured and sketched the window and door placements. Using an Exacto blade, I cut away rectangles of cardboard to form window and door openings. With the  same type of cardboard, I fashioned decorative window frames and doors and then glued plastic cellophane in place to act as window glass. The four walls were glued to a base of stiff cardboard and assembled vertically to become the model's east, west, north, and south sides of the house. Other decorative elements, were drawn, cut out, decorated and fashioned to the exterior walls of the house. These included the front porch; including grandmother's flower trellises, the back door step, the back wood shed, electrical meter box, mother's clothes stand, a garbage can, and even a shovel, a rake, a garden hoe, and a pitchfork to hang from the side wall of the wood shed!

Before the roof pieces could be placed atop the walls and glued into place, all of the interior elements needed to be considered. Again, returning to my famous notebook and all those measurements, I sketched out the interior floors, ceiling, and wall pieces. Those got wallpapered, painted, or tiled. Completing these pieces enabled me to construct the downstairs interior rooms of the little house. Next, the process included the design and insertion of important items like the staircase and the kitchen cupboards. These were constructed of the same light cardboard, cut out, painted, fashioned, and glued into place. The first floor furnishing, appliances, and adornments were to be tackled next. Carefully using cardboard, cotton batten, and tissue paper, everything from the Gauthier's real home was crafted in miniature. These items included: chairs and tables, fridge and stove, washing machine, couches and easy chairs, cabinets, and draperies to name just a few of the things made in miniature. Each miniature was glued into place to match the look and style of the real kitchen, back kitchen or den, and front room or parlour. The final touch for the downstairs was the gluing into place of the cardboard ceiling, in which I had embedded tiny wires and battery light bulbs that would be connected to a battery pack at a later time.

Much of the same processes described above were used to create the rooms, walls, furnishing and adornments for the upstairs floor. Pieces of cardboard

were used to form the three upstairs bedrooms, a space for the hall closet at the top of the stairs, and a space for the bathroom. These pieces were designed and glued into place. The primary 2nd floor furniture was crafted to include a few double beds, a twin bed, and a set of bunk beds. Accompanying these were dressers and clothing cupboards. As well, tissue paper curtains were trimmed and hung in the tiny windows. As it was with the first floor, the second floor now also received its ceiling and tiny ceiling light fixtures featuring the same hidden wires. The battery wiring for

both floors could now be finally connected together and affixed to the battery pack. All mini lights in the house would work with a simple slide switch to turn on or off lighting in each room. Once the roof pieces were glued into place the tiny rooms would become dark. The ability to light the rooms would enable the viewer to peer into the little rooms with ease so that she or he could appreciate the miniature fixtures inside. To complete the house, all that remained was the gluing of the roof! So, on went the roof, its soffit trims and the mock oil furnace chimney!

By the end of August after the addition of its roof, my project, more importantly my gift for my parents had been fully completed. I wrapped it gently in coloured tissue paper and hid it secretly at the top of our wardrobe cupboard upstairs in the boys' room until time for its presentation to Mom and Dad. After a celebration meal that we had prepared for our parents in honour of their anniversary on September 7th, I presented them with their gift. My father smiled with surprise and pride and my mother wept tears. They kept this keepsake in their home and treasured it for many years. After both Mom and Dad had passed away, my brothers gave it back to me to keep as a family heirloom. Today, I have it proudly displayed in our home and do take it out of its glass case at

Christmastime and do use it as one of my most cherished Christmas ornaments. I have added tiny battery Christmas lights around its roof and front veranda, giving it a festive look when lit. When I look at it, I ponder and remember fondly my parents, my siblings, our grandmother, and the wonderful times we had growing up in that house in Otter Lake Quebec.

In closing dear reader, I am wondering if you are asking yourself if the smallest house in Otter Lake has plumbing and a bathroom. Well, though the big house did indeed have both indoor plumbing and an upstairs bathroom, the answer to your question is no! The smallest house in Otter Lake has no toilet!!

Lastly, who lived there? Possibly a lady bug or two, but unlikely!!

Crafting the 12 Days of Christmas

In 1975, I was a ten year old boy. In early December of that year, my head was filled with dreams and visions of the upcoming Christmas season. In my view, the  holiday season brought so much warmth and joy  to everyone. The joy was evident with the friendly gesture of simply saying Merry Christmas to someone, resulting in their bright eyes shining and sporting a wide smile. There are some Grinches and Scrooges, but then again the world is not a perfect place!

At this young age, I was very interested in crafts of every kind. I adored making Christmas decorations and homemade presents for those I held dear. I could dream up tons of ideas on my own, but  often I got my inspiration from something special  that my mother would give to me nearly each Christmas season. Almost each December, my mother would buy and give to me a holiday craft magazine that she picked up on one of her trips to Shawville, Quebec or to Renfrew, Ontario. That particular year, she gifted me with the latest copy of McCalls Christmas Make-It Ideas magazine!

Oh what Joy! I thanked Mom and immediately opened this treasure to discover all possibilities inside. Luckily, in the background someone was playing a Christmas album on our old record player. This established the right mood, and at that moment I felt very cheery and festive! The current melody tickling my ears was one of my favourites. It was "The Twelve Days of Christmas".  I started to hum along and lo and behold,  as I flipped through my new magazine, the next page brightly displayed plans to cut and sew together a Twelve Days of Christmas banner! I loved it! This banner was going to be my craft project this Christmas. There was however, one tiny problem; I did not know how to sew! What did this boy of 10 years old do? Well he consulted with the experts!

I was very fortunate, because both of my grandmothers, my mother, and my aunts were expert quilt makers, and those fine ladies sure knew how to sew! My mother in fact, was a very talented seamstress. I have the fondest memories of my paternal grandmother cutting out beautiful quilt pieces   selected from her bags of scrap fabric, patiently sewing each together into fantastic designs, then stretching out the finished quilt top onto a large wooden frame, and then sewing it all, quilting it all, by hand into intricate designs, one stitch at a time, until the whole quilt was completed. I retain vivid happy memories of my mother sitting excitedly in front of her sewing machine whizzing together yet another beautiful dress, or outfit, or shirt, or pants, or designer garment; that rapidly came together from the varied fabric pieces she had made and cut out from her very own brown paper bag patterns.

After consulting Mom and Granny Gauthier, I was very happy that they were willing to share their knowledge, secrets, and skill which related to sewing. Mom helped me gather the tools. I needed sewing needles, pins, strong thread, carbon paper to make a transfer pattern from my magazine, an embroidery hoop to keep my fabric pieces taught while I sewed, and of course a selection of bright and

colourful fabrics! Mom gave me permission to choose any fabric I wanted from her rag bag. I dumped the bag and found a beautiful old baby blue satin dress. I put that piece aside for use. This first bit of blue fabric gave me the inspiration to choose other similar pieces of cloth to complement it. To accompany the beautiful blue, I then chose other scraps of green, white, pink, gold, brown, red, yellow, and violet, all of which were made of silk, satin, or some other shiny elegant fabric. The former garments from which these pieces came from were old dresses, scarves, blouses, slacks, coat linings, and even yes, even some pairs of ladies underwear!

Next, Mom showed me how to use carbon tracing paper to transfer the designs from the McCalls pages to bits of cardboard. Once, I had my very own pattern pieces drawn and cut out, I then was able to use these cardboard patterns, and a trusty pencil to trace out the shapes and pieces I needed on the varied bits of selected

fabric. Having everything clearly and sharply traced made it very easy to cut out all of the fabric pieces that I needed to assemble for each of the Twelve Days of Christmas for my banner. My dear mother was an excellent teacher that day, because not one drop of blood was put upon these pretty pieces of silk or satin from any cuts or pricks to my tiny fingers!

Now came the hard part. I needed to actually learn how to sew! For this task, it was my Granny that I turned to and it was she who became my teacher. I soon learned that sewing was not just sewing, but it also included unraveling thread and threading needles! According to Granny, my young eyes were perfect for treading needles, and from that day forward she deputized me as her "Official Needle Threader"! The job started by placing and pinning the cut-outs into their proper place. This needed to be done with care to ensure that the selected pieces did indeed make up one of the scenes of the Twelve Days of Christmas! Would it not be funny if the "Ten Maids a Milking" were milking geese instead of cows?! Each little piece got

carefully secured to the bigger affixed piece of fabric that was now tightly held in Mom's large embroidery hoop. Now, came the needle and thread part. A long piece of thread was cut from its spool. One of its ends was carefully threaded through the head of the needle. The thread then got pulled through the needle, stretching it tight ensuring the both of its ends eventually met together. Granny then instructed that we needed to tie a tight baby knot at the ends by looping the tiny thread ends around my finger and pulling them back through the loop. I struggled but, after Granny demonstrated the technique a few more times, I finally got it!

Stitching the pieces of fabric firmly to the background cloth was the next task to be mastered. From underneath, Granny pushed the needle through the background textile and then pulled it all the way through to a point where the tiny, tiny knot caught in the fabric. She then plunged the needle back through the fabric in the opposite direction, but this time taking caution to ensure she had caught the cut-out fabric piece she was now stitching into place. She then looked up and smiled at me as she said "So, Ricky, do you understand how to do it?" I responded, "Yes, Granny may I try?" She chuckled, "You most certainly can try child, because you will have about 6000 more stitches to make!" She finished her sentence with one of her "Oh Good Golly!" laughs! I thanked Granny for her help and started stitching away, a little bit every day, until I had completed the panels for each of the

Twelve Days of Christmas! Now you may ask, "Was my stitching as beautifully done as my grandmother's"? "No, of course not", I would reply to you! My grandmother was a veteran at the craft and kept her work neat and tight. Mine at times admittedly was a bit sloppier! Well, I did the best I could as a 10 year old child! You see, my focus was not always on my handiwork, but sometime drifted away to Santa, gifts, and eating some of the Christmas cookies and squares that my Mom had been baking! A few missed stitches really should not matter that much, right?!!!!

All 12 panels for my banner were now complete, pressed flat, and cut so that they formed equal, well nearly equal squares! With my mother's help and the magic of her big electric sewing machine, we patched the frames together into two rows. After that, the two rows were sewn together with a tight neat seam up the middle. Mom then used some of the same beautiful blue satin fabric and framed my banner by stitching an attractive blue border all around it. Mother expertly designed a loop at the top in which she slid a thin dowel stick and a strong piece of string that she had saved from an old hanging calendar. After one more final pressing, and my mother directing me to go put away the iron and ironing board, Mom excitedly asked me as to where was I going to hang it up? I quickly decided that it should hang at the bottom of the staircase, so that I could see it each morning when I descended the stairs during the Christmas season.

This Christmas banner depicting the Twelve Days of Christmas adorned our stairwell each year for as long as I lived with my family in Otter Lake, Quebec. It was stored away each year with the other Christmas decorations, which allowed it to remain in very good shape. When I moved away from home, my mother returned this banner to me one year wrapped up as one of my very special Christmas gifts from her. Each year since, it has been joyfully hung in any place I called home from early December to the Epiphany celebrations of Little Christmas. Each season it is brought out of my storage locker, ironed, and hung up. Each Christmastime, I look upon it and I say "Thank you Granny, thank you Mom, Merry Christmas Everyone."

ABOUT THE AUTHOR

Rick J.M. Gauthier -
rickjmgauthier@sympatico.ca

Rick, a humble small town guy, is now a retired public servant who is using his skills to recount heartwarming short stories, born from cherished childhood memories. He loves history and enjoys theatre, music, and audio books. He hopes to continue creating short stories and volunteering to help the elderly.

Manufactured by Amazon.ca
Bolton, ON